P9-DMW-332

Rattlestiltskin

by Eric A. Kimmel

Illustrated by Erin Camarca

WESTWINDS
PRESS®

Para Carrol y David y Dani en Guadalajara —E. K.
For Roan —E. C

Text © 2016 by Eric A. Kimmel
Illustrations © 2016 by Erin Camarca

All rights reserved. No part of this book may be reproduced or transmitted in any form or by any means, electronic or mechanical, including photocopying, recording, or by any information storage and retrieval system, without written permission of the publisher.

Library of Congress Cataloging-in-Publication Data

Names: Kimmel, Eric A., author. | Camarca, Erin, illustrator.
Title: Rattlestiltskin / by Eric A. Kimmel ; illustrated by Erin Camarca. Description: Portland, Oregon :
WestWinds Press, [2016] | Summary: In this Southwestern version of Rumplestiltskin, Rosalinda is
in debt to the strange little snake man Rattlestiltskin after he teaches her how to make tortillas so
light they float in the air, but can she outsmart the trickster and keep her freedom?
Identifiers: LCCN 2015034596 | ISBN 9781943328383 (hardcover) ISBN 9781943328390 (e-book)
Subjects: | CYAC: Fairy tales. | Folklore—Germany. Classification: LCC PZ8.K527 Rat 2016 | DDC 398.2—dc23
LC record available at http://lccn.loc.gov/2015034596

Editor: Michelle McCann
Designer: Vicki Knapton

Published by WestWinds Press® An imprint of

GRAPHIC ARTS
BOOKS®

P.O. Box 56118 Portland, Oregon 97238-6118
503-254-5591
www.graphicartsbooks.com
Printed in China

Making tortillas is an art. Oh, yes, you can buy tortillas in the store. However, they're just not the same as ones lovingly made by hand; thin as flower petals and light as baby's breath.

M y daughter Rosalia makes the best tortillas," Señora Gonzales told her friends after church. "They are so light, they float like clouds."

"*¡No manches!* Come on! You're telling stories," Señora Mendoza said. "Even I can't make tortillas like that. And everyone knows my tortillas are the best in town."

"*Were* the best," Señora Gonzales said.

"*¡Hijole!* Indeed!"

Everyone turned to see who had spoken. It was Don Ignacio, *El Patrón*, the richest man in town. "I love tortillas," Don Ignacio said. "I have searched all my life for the perfect tortilla. If your daughter's tortillas really float like clouds, her fortune is made. Send her to my hacienda tomorrow. I wish to see what she can do."

"¡Ay, mamá! Why did you tell such lies?" Rosalia cried when she learned what had happened.

"Your tortillas *almost* float, *mija*," Rosalia's mother said. "Just make them a little thinner and maybe they will. Go to the hacienda and try your best. *Que será, será.* What will be, will be."

Rosalia knocked on the hacienda door. Don Ignacio greeted her. He led her outside to an adobe oven. A table held mixing bowls, masa, water, a griddle—everything she needed to make tortillas.

C all me when the tortillas arc done. I want to see them float," said Don Ignacio.

"What if they don't?" Rosalia asked.

"¡*Aguas!* Watch out! They'd better, for your sake. I don't like braggarts. Or liars." Don Ignacio then left, leaving Rosalia alone.

"What if I fail? Will he make me walk across the desert barefoot? Will he stick me full of cactus spines? Will he make me eat hot chili peppers until smoke comes out my nose? *¡Ay, ay, ay!* Better get busy."

Rosalia started making tortillas. They were light and as thin as she could make them, but none of them floated. Rosalia didn't know what to do.

"Please, *mis tortillitas!* Float!" she cried.

"*¿Qué onda, chava?* What's going on? You want your tortillas to float? They'll float . . . if you really want them to."

A strange little man popped out of the oven. He was as short as a stump and dressed in rattlesnake skins. The buttons on his clothes were rattlesnake rattles. They rattled and buzzed as he spoke.

"I can make floating tortillas," the stranger said, brushing off the cinders. "*No hay problema*. It's no problem at all. What will you do for me if I teach you the secret?"

"I'll do anything you ask," Rosalia said.

"It's a deal," said the little snake man with a wicked grin.

He whispered a few words in her ear. Then the two set to work. Within minutes, tortillas were floating in the air. The little snake man tipped his hat and climbed back in the oven.

"*Hasta luego.* See you later," he said. "Remember your promise."

Don Ignacio was amazed to see the floating tortillas.
He ate them all, though it was difficult to keep them on his plate.
He told Rosalia, "Come live here at the hacienda. You'll be rich.
You won't have to do anything but make tortillas."

"I'd like that," Rosalia said.

Rosalia moved into the hacienda. She enjoyed living in beautiful rooms, wearing lovely clothes, and having servants wait on her day and night. Rosalia was so happy.

All she had to do was make floating tortillas whenever Don Ignacio's friends came by. That was easy, now that she knew the secret. She completely forgot about the little snake man.

Then one day she looked up and there he was. "What do you want?" Rosalia asked.

He pointed a snaky finger at her. "YOU!"

"Me? Why?"

"Me and my brothers live in a shack out in the cactus," the little snake man said. "We're tired of living in a pigpen and wearing filthy clothes. We're tired of making our own tortillas, whether or not they float. We want a maid to keep house for us—to cook our food and wash the floor and mend our socks and scrub our dirty underwear. You're the one!"

"No, I'm not! Find someone else," Rosalia said.

"You promised!" the little snake man said.

"No, I didn't! You tricked me!"

"A promise is a promise. But just to be fair, I'll give you three chances to guess my name. If you can do it, I'll go away and never come back. *¿Ahora, cómo me llamo?* Now, what's my name?"

Rosalia looked the little snake man over.

"Is it Hernando?"

"No. That's one."

"Is it Guillermo?"

"That's two."

"Is it Alejandro?"

"That's three. You didn't guess it. *Ven conmigo.* Let's go."

"That wasn't fair at all!" Rosalia said. "You hardly gave me time to think. I want three more guesses."

"*¡Calmate!* Take it easy. It won't help you," the little snake man said. "I'll come by tomorrow. See you then. *Hasta luego.*"

Rosalia tried to answer, "*Hasta la vista.*" But the words stuck in her throat.

Rosalia spent the next day in the library studying a book of names.
The door opened and the little snake man walked in.

"What's my name?" he said.

Rosalia turned the pages of her book. "Is your name Procopio?"

"That's one."

"Is your name Rigoberto?"

"That's two."

"Is your name Mayahuel?"

"That's three. You used up your guesses.

¡Vámonos! Let's go."

"*¡Un momentito!* Just a minute!" Rosalia replied. "There are thousands of names. Six guesses isn't enough. You have to give me another chance."

"Another, but no more," the little snake man said. "If you can't guess my name tomorrow, you're coming with me. *Hasta mañana.*"

Poor Rosalia. She had only three guesses left.

Rosalia decided to run away. Maybe she could find somewhere
to hide where the little snake man could never find her.
She left the hacienda before dawn. Rosalia walked and walked,
and by the time the sun went down, she was way out in the desert.

The only building for miles around was a tumbledown shack.
  She heard a fiddle playing. Maybe the fiddler would help her get
to the next town.
    Rosalia walked up to the shack. The fiddling grew louder.
Rosalia peeked in the window.

She saw two dozen little men having a square dance. The fiddler stood on a table, stomping his foot as he called out the steps. It was the little snake man.

"Promenade and don't be slow.
What's my name?
I'll bet you know.
Shout the answer,
loud and plain . . ."

All the little men yelled together.

"Rattlestiltskin! That's your name!"

"So that's his name!" said Rosalia. "Rattlestiltskin!"

"Someone's peeking in the window!" one of the little men cried. They poured out of the shack, chasing after Rosalia.

But Rosalia could run fast. She soon left the little men behind. She ran until she saw the lights of the hacienda. As she ran, she said the word over and over again with each step so she wouldn't forget.

"Ratttlestiltskin . . . Rattlestiltskin . . . Rattlestiltskin . . ."

That evening Rosalia was sitting by the window when who came through the door but the little snake man.

"Last three guesses. What's my name?"

Rosalia took a deep breath. "Oh, dear! Is your name . . . Garcilaso?"

"That's one."

"Is your name . . . Rodrigo?"

"That's two. Let's go!"

"I still have one more guess," Rosalia said. She closed her eyes tight. "Is your name . . ."

"Rattlestiltskin??!!"

The little snake man stomped his feet. His rattlesnake buttons began buzzing. "How did you know? Somebody told you!"

"Never mind how I know," Rosalia said. "I guessed your name. Our business is done. *No quejes tanto.* Stop complaining. And don't slam the door on your way out."

But the little snake man didn't go out the door. His cheeks puffed out and his hair stood up. He began rattling and buzzing until he rattled and buzzed himself to pieces.

An empty snakeskin was all that remained.

Rosalia never saw the little snake man again. Don Ignacio and all his friends agreed that Rosalia made the best tortillas in the land, even if they were hard to keep on a plate. Mama moved into the hacienda and she and Rosalia lived happily ever after.

As for the little snake man, some say he's still around. Folks claim to run into him from time to time. If *you* ever do, be careful making promises. And keep in mind the words to that song.

Promenade and don't be slow.
What's his name? I'll bet you know.
Shout the answer, loud and plain . . .
Rattlestiltskin is his name.

Rosalia made her tortillas the traditional way.
Here's an easier recipe you can try yourself.

Homemade Tortillas

3 cups unbleached flour
1 teaspoon salt
½ teaspoon baking powder

⅓ cup vegetable oil
1 cup hot water

Mix the flour, salt, and baking powder together. Add the oil. Mix together. Add hot water. Knead until the dough forms a ball. Cover and let rest for 30 minutes. Divide the dough into 12 even-sized balls. Roll them out one at a time on a floured surface. Cook on a hot, ungreased pan over medium high heat. Turn the tortilla over when brown blisters form. Cook on the other side. Serve warm.

(For safety's sake, children should always have an adult present when cooking on a hot stove.)